YEARLING BOOKS/YOUNG YEARLINGS/YEARLING CLASSICS are designed especially to entertain and enlighten young people. Patricia Reilly Giff, consultant to this series, received her bachelor's degree from Marymount College and a master's degree in history from St. John's University. She holds a Professional Diploma in Reading and a Doctorate of Humane Letters from Hofstra University. She was a teacher and reading consultant for many years, and is the author of numerous books for young readers.

For a complete listing of all Yearling titles, write to
Dell Readers Service, P.O. Box 1045,
South Holland, IL 60473.

THE "JINGLE BELLS" JAM

Patricia Reilly Giff

Illustrated by
Emily Arnold McCully

A YOUNG YEARLING BOOK

Published by
DELL PUBLISHING
a division of
Bantam Doubleday Dell Publishing Group, Inc.
666 Fifth Avenue
New York, New York 10103

The trademark Yearling® is registered in the U.S. Patent and Trademark Office.

The trademark Dell® is registered in the U.S. Patent and Trademark Office.

ISBN 0-440-40534-3

Printed in the United States of America

November 1992

10 9 8 7 6 5 4 3 2 1

*To
Raina Liepins,
with love*

♪ CHAPTER 1 ♪

Boom. Boom. Boom.

Crash.

The sound was all around her.

Chrissie Tripp's ears rang.

The boom was Kinesha Brown on the big bass drum.

Crash again.

That was Nathan Thomas on the cymbals.

Lucky Kinesha. Lucky Nathan.

Anyone could bang away on a bass drum.

Anyone could smash a pair of cymbals together.

Just let them try jiggling their fingers around a fife and make it come out sounding like "Jingle Bells."

Chrissie grinned. Never mind. She loved being in the Lincoln Lions Band.

"Rum dum dum," she mumbled in time with the drums.

She loved swinging her arms, breathing deep, taking big steps . . . even when it was up and down the schoolyard, practicing, the way they were right now.

Professor Thurman was marching along next to the junior band. They called him Professor Thum-de-dum. His lips were moving. "Pom pom pom."

His hair was wild and gray. His shoes went high up and were laced. He was probably a hundred and two.

Next to her mother and father, he was the greatest person in the whole world.

He turned and saw her looking at him.

He smiled and winked.

Chrissie smiled back.

She straightened up as tall as she could.

She wanted him to think she was a terrific marcher.

He smiled at her once more, then speeded up to march with the seniors in front.

Chrissie looked at everyone's feet in her line.

She took a skip.

Sometimes she had a little trouble keeping in step with the rest of the band.

"Left-right-left-right-left-right-left," she tried to recite in her head.

Still she came down on the wrong foot.

And that worm-faced Jessica Martinez knew it.

Just because Jessica was the leader of the junior band, she thought she was king of the world.

Snap, snap went Jessica's fingers.

You couldn't hear the snap, of course. But you could see that skinny arm come out. You could see those snaky fingers pointing right at Chrissie's feet.

Everyone in line poked out his head to look.

Even Sarah Arlia in the row ahead turned to see what Chrissie was doing wrong.

Chrissie changed feet as fast as she could.

She felt like taking the fife and smacking Jessica on her skinny little snapping fingers.

She couldn't do that though.

Right now it was time for the fifers to play. One. Two. Three . . .

"Jingle Bells . . ." they began.

Chrissie began too.

She had practiced a couple of times.

She still couldn't get past "... all the way."

In the meantime, she wiggled her fingers up and down on the fife.

No one knew the difference. At least, she hoped they didn't.

Way up ahead, her sister, Teresa, the drum major, raised her arm.

They were going to do "to the rear, march" ... otherwise they'd bang right into the schoolyard wall.

Chrissie got ready to spin around.

Teresa's arm came down.

She spun.

So did everyone else.

Chrissie spun too far.

"Oof," said Michelle Swoop next to her.

"Sorry," Chrissie mouthed.

They started down the schoolyard the other way.

They had done that about fifty-eight times today.

Each time, Chrissie had looked at the backyards on the other side of the fence.

Mrs. Aiello's, Mrs. Champion's, her own house, and Mrs. Niebling's . . . the crankiest person on the block.

Chrissie could see her cat, Thankly, up on the fence.

He was walking on top, keeping up with the band. His tail was stuck straight in the air, with just the tiniest curve on the end.

The curve was from the time Chrissie had slammed the bedroom door by accident.

Snap went Jessica Martinez's fingers.

Chrissie gave another skip.

Up in front Teresa blew her whistle again.

"Halt," she screamed.

Chrissie banged into Sarah Arlia.

From behind, Ahmed banged into Chrissie. Willie banged into Ahmed.

Nathan crashed the cymbals together again.

Then everything was still.

For a moment Chrissie's ears kept ringing.

Then she could hear Willie laughing somewhere in back of her.

Professor Thum-de-dum shook his head a little. His wild gray hair waved in the air. "A surprise," he said. "The band is going to play Christmas carols at the Sunrise Mall. A week from Saturday afternoon."

Chrissie and Michelle Swoop looked at each other.

Terrific.

"So . . ." said the professor. "I hope the fifers know 'Jingle Bells' perfectly."

He smoothed his hair down a little. "Nothing like 'Jingle Bells' on the fife."

Chrissie stood very still in her place.

Was the professor looking at her? Did he

know she was making believe when she played?

She looked straight in front of her, at the bow in Sarah Arlia's hair.

She tried to act as if she knew "Jingle Bells" perfectly . . . as perfectly as Michelle Swoop did.

And Michelle certainly knew "Jingle Bells." She could play almost anything. Maybe that was because she was the professor's granddaughter.

"DIS-MISSED," screeched Teresa.

Everyone scattered across the yard.

Chrissie dashed around the professor.

"Great marching," he called after her.

She ducked her head, feeling wonderful. "Thanks."

She was going to learn "Jingle Bells."

She had to . . . if it was the last thing she ever did.

♪ CHAPTER 2 ♪

Chrissie raced for the deli. Behind her Willie was racing too.

Leave it to Willie to figure out she had a couple of quarters.

She stopped to wait for him. Then they went inside together.

Mrs. Serio had decorated the whole store for Christmas. Cardboard reindeer were all over the place.

A dish of free hard candy was on the counter.

It looked exactly like last year's candy.

Chrissie took a red one. It even tasted dusty. "Four whistle pops, please," she said around the candy.

"Baby stuff," said Willie. "How about banana sticks?"

"My money," said Chrissie.

"It's Christmas," said Mrs. Serio. "Better to give than receive."

"Right." Willie grinned.

Chrissie rolled her eyes. "Two whistle pops, then. And two banana sticks."

"That's the spirit," said Mrs. Serio.

Chrissie was dying to get rid of the hard candy in her mouth.

She didn't want to hurt Mrs. Serio's feelings though.

She rolled it between her cheek and her teeth, trying not to taste it. Then she put her money on the counter and took the bag. "Thanks."

Joseph and his girlfriend, Alysia, stopped outside the window to look at the cardboard reindeer.

"Come on, Willie." Chrissie shoved a banana stick at him and raced out.

She fished in her mouth for the red candy, put it in her pocket, and blew on a whistle pop, hard.

It sounded like Thankly yeowling.

Joseph turned around and stared at them.

He made motions with his hands. Go-away motions.

He turned and kept walking. He never stopped talking to Alysia.

"Hey, Joey. Wait up." She blasted the pop again.

He looked over his shoulder.

So did Alysia.

Joseph didn't look too friendly. "Some kids on my street," he told the girl.

Willie started to laugh.

"Don't pay attention," she told Willie. "Joseph's making believe he's Prince Charles."

Joseph and the girl turned the corner.

She and Willie crossed to the other side and started down the street.

"Have to learn that 'Jingle Bells,'" Chrissie said. "Have to."

"That's easy," said Willie.

Chrissie bit a chunk off her pop. It wasn't easy. Not one bit easy.

"Love it on the drums," said Willie. "A rum-dum-pum. A rum-dum-pum."

He hit imaginary cymbals together.

They passed the professor's house.

The professor's wife was at the window. She was hanging a Christmas angel. She waved to them.

They waved back. Willie was still jumping around, playing the drums.

"Gotta listen to it," Willie said. "Get the beat of it."

Chrissie didn't answer. Never mind the beat. She couldn't even get the right sound on the fife.

They turned the corner. They passed Mrs. Niebling's gray-and-white house.

Mrs. Niebling was out in front, picking dead leaves out of her garden.

They speeded up to get past.

Mrs. Niebling always had something to say.

Something miserable.

"Christine Elizabeth," Mrs. Niebling called. "I've been looking for you."

Chrissie sighed.

Mrs. Niebling didn't like kids. She especially didn't like Chrissie.

Chrissie had picked her flowers last year.

She had picked them for her mother.

Mrs. Niebling had acted as if she had set her house on fire. "They're irises," she had said. "Prize irises."

Now Mrs. Niebling called her again. "Chris-tine."

Chrissie took a breath.

"See you," Willie said. He kept going.

Some friend.

Chrissie took a step up Mrs. Niebling's path.

Mrs. Niebling had on her worst face. "Christine," she said. "Your cat—"

"Thankly?" Chrissie could see Thankly coming up behind Mrs. Niebling.

She hoped he wouldn't rub against her neighbor's ankles.

Mrs. Niebling might have a stroke or something.

Chrissie clicked her fingers quietly.

Mrs. Niebling went on. "Whatever her name is—"

"He," said Christine. "He's a he."

Mrs. Niebling waved her hand in the air. "It's bad enough he sleeps on my irises all spring. But now he's sleeping under my bird feeder. The birds can't even eat in peace."

"Sorry," Chrissie said.

Thankly sat down, an inch behind Mrs. Niebling.

He started to wash one paw.

Chrissie cleared her throat.

Thankly looked up at her. He began to wash again.

The cat was impossible.

"It has to stop," said Mrs. Niebling. "Keep that cat home."

"Thankly wanders around all over the place. It's hard—"

Mrs. Niebling clicked her teeth. "I mean it, Chrissie. I won't have him eating my birds."

"Don't step back," Chrissie said.

Mrs. Niebling looked over her shoulder.

She saw Thankly. "I can't stand this another minute." She waved the end of her coat. "Shoo."

Chrissie leaned over. She scooped Thankly up.

The cat dug one claw into Chrissie's neck. He didn't like to be bossed around.

She hurried down the street. The whole time, Thankly struggled to get away.

Chrissie stopped at her own front steps and reached for the knob.

Her mother had hung a wreath on the door.

Chrissie pressed her face against it.

It smelled like the woods last summer.

It smelled like Christmas.

Even Thankly took a couple of sniffs.

She opened the door and let Thankly jump out of her arms.

Teresa had beaten her home. She was sitting in the living room, doing math.

The whole place was a mess with boxes

of ornaments. The tree was bare, waiting to be decorated.

Chrissie looped the gold roping around her neck.

Then she rooted through one of the boxes.

"Do you have to do that now?" Teresa asked. "I'm trying to do my homework."

"Here it is," Chrissie said. She held up an ornament. "My favorite."

It was a silver lady with a basket of blue flowers. Mrs. Johnson, her kindergarten teacher, had given it to her because she had gotten chicken pox that Christmas. "Look, Teresa."

Teresa wasn't listening. She tapped her pencil against her teeth.

Chrissie looked closer. The flowers were just like Mrs. Niebling's.

She put the ornament back. She right-flanked into the kitchen.

Thankly was there . . . still washing the

same paw. But now he was sitting on a plate in the middle of the table.

"You're in enough trouble, Thankly." She picked him up and set him on the floor.

A piece of crumb cake was left on the plate. It was a little squashed. She dusted it off and crammed it into her mouth.

The front door opened.

It was Joseph.

"Wait till I get my hands on that kid," he told Teresa. "Red candy stuff all over her mouth. Following me around . . ."

"Blah, blah," Chrissie told Thankly. She narrowed her eyes. "People I'm sick of: One, Mrs. Niebling. Two, Joseph."

"Will you stop talking to yourself," Teresa yelled in. "I can't concentrate."

"Three, Teresa."

♪ CHAPTER 3 ♪

Chrissie looked at the clock.

The hands didn't move.

It was going to stay at two-thirty forever.

Mrs. Lovejoy was doing something called young authors . . . something called brain-storming for ideas.

Chrissie wished she could brainstorm herself right out of the classroom.

She stood up and went to the pencil sharpener.

"I see you're using up your pencil," Mrs. Lovejoy said. "But I hope you're thinking of ideas too."

"I am, really," said Chrissie. She tried to look as if she were crazy about brainstorming.

"Would you like to help us then?" Mrs. Lovejoy asked.

Chrissie looked up at the blackboard.

Lines and circles were all over the place.

Mrs. Lovejoy kept scribbling in ideas.

Chrissie couldn't think of one idea.

She could see Willie looking at her. His eyes were opened wide.

She looked at Mrs. Lovejoy, then back to him.

He had pulled his cheeks in. It looked as if he were having an attack of some kind.

"Uh . . . sick," Chrissie told Mrs. Lovejoy.

Mrs. Lovejoy frowned.

Willie was shaking his head, hard.

"Uh . . ."

He was saying something. It looked like deli.

She leaned over.

"Willie," said Mrs. Lovejoy. "I never can figure out how you have so much to say when you're not supposed to. Then when I ask . . ."

Willie looked as if he were going to laugh.

"Stand up, please," Mrs. Lovejoy told him.

"I was just trying to help," Willie said.

Mrs. Lovejoy sighed. "All right. Give us some help."

"How about doing a story that tells why it's better to give than receive?"

Mrs. Lovejoy looked surprised.

She stared at Willie for a minute. "Excellent," she said. "Excellent idea."

Then the bell rang.

Mrs. Lovejoy nodded.

Everyone raced for jackets and hats.

Two minutes later, they were out the classroom door.

"I can't believe it," Chrissie told Willie.

Willie drummed his books on the stair rail. Rat-a-tat-tat. "I can't believe it either," he said.

It was freezing outside, gray and windy. Chrissie buried her face in her scarf.

"I remembered the deli," said Willie. "Mrs. Serio."

"That's what you were telling me, and I was supposed to figure out . . ."

Willie sucked in his cheeks. "The whistle pops, remember?"

They turned the corner. "Good grief," Chrissie said.

"I tried," said Willie.

Chrissie shook her head. "No. I don't mean that."

She pointed.

She could see Thankly's tail disappearing around the side of Mrs. Niebling's house.

She dashed down the street.

Willie dashed after her.

At the end of Mrs. Niebling's driveway she stopped on one foot. "Not a sound," she told Willie.

They tiptoed up the driveway.

Chrissie could see lights in Mrs. Niebling's living room.

It looked warm inside.

She shivered.

Chrissie could see Mrs. Niebling inside, decorating her Christmas tree.

She was reaching up, looping lights over the branches.

She was all by herself.

Chrissie pictured her family putting up their tree.

Her mother always made hot cider; and

there were cookies, homemade, with sprinkles or cherries.

Chrissie tiptoed into Mrs. Niebling's yard.

Thankly was sitting under the bird feeder.

He was watching a bird eat.

The bird kept scattering seed off the tray.

Thankly kept reaching with one paw, trying to catch the seed.

Chrissie tiptoed toward him.

Willie fell over the stones at the edge of the path.

The bird flew.

Thankly loped after it.

Chrissie made a dash after the cat.

Too late. He flattened himself under the fence and disappeared into Mrs. Aiello's backyard.

"Thanks, Willie," Chrissie said.

She could hear Mrs. Niebling's back door open.

"Run," she whispered.

They hopped over the stone path and headed for home.

Chrissie looked back.

Mrs. Niebling hadn't seen them.

She was emptying a fresh cup of seed into the feeder.

Chrissie took a breath.

She hoped Thankly would stay in Mrs. Aiello's yard until Mrs. Niebling went back into her house again.

♪ CHAPTER 4 ♪

On Saturday Chrissie sat in her bedroom. The music sheet lay on the floor in front of her.

She curled her fingers around the fife.

Ready, she told herself.

"Nice, even breath," the professor always said. "Otherwise, the fife will squeak."

Chrissie gave it her best even breath.

"Jin-gle bells . . ."

Squeaky.

Her bedroom door burst open.

It was Joseph. His face was covered with white lotion.

"What's that stuff?" Chrissie asked.

"That fife . . ." Joseph said at the same time.

She turned her head to one side. "What song? If you were guessing?"

Joseph looked up at the ceiling. "Song? It sounded like 'squeak squeak squeak.'"

"Very good, Joseph," she said. "Now I know why you can't do algebra. You have the brains of a frog."

Joseph laughed. "'Jingle Bells.' I knew it all the time."

"Really?" Joseph wasn't so bad. Not nearly as bad as Teresa.

"Your face," Chrissie began again. "What . . . ?"

Joseph touched his cheek with one finger. "For acne. I've got to look good. I have a part-time job. I'm going to be a stock boy at Bradley's department store."

Chrissie blinked. Joseph was the laziest kid in the world.

"Got to get a present for Alysia Link," Joseph said. "Spring Flowers . . ."

"Nice," Chrissie said. She had half a bottle of that in her drawer. They should have called it Stink Flowers.

She listened as he went down the hall. Then she started to practice again.

She sighed. She was terrible.

The front doorbell rang.

Her bedroom was in front of the house, her window on top of the door.

In the summertime, she could open the screen.

She could spit down on someone if she wanted.

She never did, even though it was a great idea.

The bell rang again.

Nobody in this house ever bothered to answer it.

She wiped at the steamy windowpane.

Outside it had started to snow.

She loved the snow. She loved to get her face down close to it, to smell its wet coldness.

The bell rang for the third time.

Good grief.

Then she heard her mother's footsteps.

"Chrissie, it's for you."

Chrissie ran her sleeve over her face and headed downstairs.

Michelle Swoop was in the hall, stamping her boots. "It's snowing out," she said.

Michelle had a long face with lots of curly brown hair. She had pink glasses.

Poor Michelle was ugly as a snake . . . except when she smiled. When she smiled, she looked great.

"Want to go Christmas shopping?" Michelle asked. "Christmas looking, I mean. I don't have any money."

"I'm working on the fife," Chrissie said slowly. "I can't seem to . . ."

Michelle leaned forward. "You have to hear it in your head. The music, I mean." She frowned. "It's hard to explain."

Chrissie waved her arm. "Don't worry."

She went into the kitchen.

Her mother was stirring something in a pot. It smelled like dog food.

Chrissie took a breath. "All right if I go to Bradley's with Michelle?"

"Sure." Her mother took a spoonful out of the pot and tasted it. "Hideous."

"I thought so," Chrissie said.

Her mother stared down at the pot. "Maybe I could add some curry, or carrots."

Chrissie shuddered. She went down the hall again, pulling on her jacket.

Teresa was just coming in the door. "I have to tell you something," she said.

"I'm in a hurry." Chrissie moved around her.

"It's about Thankly."

Chrissie stopped.

Their mother poked her head out the kitchen door. "Bundle up. It's cold."

Chrissie nodded. She turned to Teresa.

Teresa shook her head. "See you later."

Chrissie and Michelle walked down the path. They held their hands out to catch the few snowflakes that were falling.

Chrissie felt a little knot of worry.

Something Teresa didn't want to tell her in front of their mother.

Something about Thankly.

Something about Mrs. Niebling?

Michelle started to cough.

"The whole world has a cold," said Chrissie.

"That's what my grandfather said." Michelle frowned. "He has a terrible cold. He had to stay in bed today."

Chrissie tried to picture the professor sick in bed.

She couldn't do it. He was always moving, always smiling.

"I hope he'll be better by the time we play at the mall," Michelle said.

Chrissie nodded. She wasn't worried.

A little cold would never get him down.

Besides, there was something else to worry about. Thankly.

A few minutes later, she and Michelle pushed open the door to Bradley's.

On the front counter were a million bottles of Spring Flowers perfume.

One of the bottles was as big as a moose.

Music was playing. It was loud, so loud she could hardly think.

The music was "Jingle Bells."

Chrissie wondered if she'd ever get past ". . . *all the way.*"

♪ CHAPTER 5 ♩

It was eleven o'clock in the morning. Mrs. Lovejoy's class was doing young authors again.

Chrissie couldn't bear to listen to one more young author.

She tiptoed out the door and went into the girls' room.

"On guard," she told the mirror.

She slashed an invisible sword in the air.

Then quickly, she looked over her shoulder to make sure no one was there.

No, it was all right.

She went over to the radiator and boosted herself up on top.

It was warm, very warm.

She had to sit on one side and keep changing legs.

It felt good, though. Today was freezing.

She turned a little to look out the window. All the roofs on the other side of the fence were white. They sparkled with frost.

Chrissie sat there for a minute. She wondered how much time she could stay out of the classroom.

Mrs. Lovejoy had a memory like an encyclopedia.

Chrissie could see her looking up. She'd say, "Christine Elizabeth Tripp has been out of this room for ten and a quarter minutes."

Chrissie slashed her sword around, thinking of the young authors in the classroom.

She should go back, but she couldn't stand it in there.

She couldn't stand listening to the stories.

They'd all had to write one for weekend homework.

The boys' were the worst.

Willie could hardly read his.

He must have copied it from something. Too bad he hadn't stuck to his better-to-give-than-receive idea.

Outside Chrissie saw something move.

She leaned her head against the window.

It was so cold she could hardly stand it.

She could see Thankly in Mrs. Niebling's yard. She looked closer.

What was he doing?

Eating something.

Good grief. It was a piece of bread.

Mrs. Niebling must have thrown bread out for the birds.

She knocked on the windowpane.

Thankly didn't look up.

It wasn't that he couldn't hear her.

Thankly could hear the sound of mackerel cat food cans being opened from seven miles away.

Chrissie thought back to Saturday . . . and Teresa talking about Thankly.

Teresa had been wrapping presents in the living room when Chrissie had come home from Bradley's.

"Don't look," said Teresa.

Chrissie shaded her eyes. "I won't."

Teresa was ahead of her in Christmas presents.

Chrissie didn't have one cent.

Chrissie was making things for everyone

instead. A pot holder for her mother. A picture of a football player for Joseph and her father.

Maybe she'd give the rest of that perfume in her drawer to Teresa.

"Don't tell Mother," Teresa began. "If Mother knows, she'll be on Mrs. Niebling's side."

Chrissie sank down on the floor.

"Mrs. Niebling caught me," said Teresa. "I was going past and she said we have to keep Thankly out of her yard. If we don't, she's going to do something about it."

Chrissie swallowed. She took the silver lady ornament out of the box and looked at it. "What does that mean?"

Teresa shook her head. "I'm not sure," she said slowly. "They might take Thankly away—"

"She couldn't do that." Chrissie felt her mouth go dry.

"I think we'd better keep Thankly in the house."

"Impossible," Chrissie said. When Thankly wanted to go out, he sneaked under the couch and waited. Sooner or later, someone would open the door.

Then he was out like a flash.

"Ouch." Right now, Chrissie raised her leg off the radiator. It was hot.

She looked out the window.

Mrs. Niebling was coming out her back door.

She was waving her arms at Thankly.

Thankly looked up.

For a moment he didn't move.

Then slowly, as if he had forever, he jumped to the top of the fence.

A moment later, he strutted across the schoolyard.

Chrissie looked back at Mrs. Niebling.

Her face was red.

Was she crying?

Never.

In back of her, the girls' room door banged open.

"Boy, are you in trouble," Michelle Swoop said. "Mrs. Lovejoy is having a fit in there."

She leaned over the sink and slurped water into her mouth.

Chrissie slid off the radiator.

She was the one who had let Thankly out this morning.

She had forgotten all about Mrs. Niebling.

Mrs. Niebling was still standing there.

Chrissie followed Michelle down the hall.

She didn't want to think about the way Mrs. Niebling looked.

♪ CHAPTER 6 ♩

"**T**oo cold for outside practice," came the message over the intercom the next Wednesday. "The Lincoln Lions Band will meet in the gym. Right after school."

For the first time, Chrissie didn't want to go to practice.

The professor wouldn't be there.

Michelle had told her he was sick, really sick. He might not even be back in time for the Sunrise Mall.

"Who's going to teach us?" Chrissie asked Michelle. "Who's going to get us ready?"

Michelle's eyes were red. "Someone else. I don't know."

After school, Chrissie followed Willie down the hall.

Willie drummed on the walls. He drummed on the floor. He even drummed on the stair rail on the way down to the gym.

They stopped at the bottom of the stairs.

Someone else was standing in front of the gym.

It was a man in a yellow shirt and blue pants.

"He looks like a parrot," Chrissie told Vernail.

"*Eek*," squawked Willie. "Flap my wings."

Teresa blew her whistle.

No one was paying attention.

She tried again, her cheeks puffed out, her face red.

Then the man with the yellow shirt stood up on the bleachers. "Don't move," he roared.

Everyone stopped still.

Everyone but Willie.

He was imitating a parrot. "Polly want a cracker," he said. "A cracker, a cracker, a . . ."

Chrissie started to laugh.

Willie was laughing too.

Yellow shirt looked at them.

Teresa blew her whistle again. "Go to your places," she screamed.

Everyone dashed for his line.

Yellow shirt waited a minute.

Then he opened his mouth. "I'm going to be here while the professor is sick," he said. "I'm Mr. Bird."

Chrissie could hear Willie explode with laughter in back.

She started to laugh too.

Mr. Bird had a long neck, a skinny neck. He really looked like a bird . . . maybe an ostrich.

Sarah Arlia turned to look at her.

Jessica Martinez was looking too.

And so was Mr. Bird.

"Is anything funny back there?" he asked.

Chrissie bit her lip.

Even his voice sounded like a bird. It was high, and a little screechy.

In back of her, Willie was trying to stop laughing.

It sounded as if he were strangling.

Teresa raised her arm. "Ready for 'Jingle Bells,' " she said.

Her arm came down.

The drums started. Pom pom pom. Pom pom pom.

Chrissie raised her fife to her mouth.

It was hard to play when her lips kept wiggling with laughter.

It didn't make any difference though.

She still didn't know "Jingle Bells" anyway.

Teresa's arm was in the air.

It came down again.

The fifers began. "Jin-gle bells, jin-gle bells . . ."

The sound of the drums was loud.

You could hardly hear the fifes or tell what the music was.

Mr. Bird was frowning.

"I want to hear the fifes," he said.

A tiny voice whispered, "Polly wants to hear the fifes."

That was Willie.

Chrissie bit her lip harder.

She stared at the floor.

Mr. Bird must have heard Willie.

He jumped off the bleachers and marched toward the junior drummers.

He stopped at Willie's row.

"Now I want to hear a drum," he said. "Let's hear how good you are."

"Me?" Willie asked.

"You," said Mr. Bird.

Willie started to play.

The sound was strange in the gym.

It almost echoed.

Willie was good though.

He was very good . . . better than some of the seniors.

"Stop," said Mr. Bird.

He came toward Chrissie.

"How about you?" he asked.

Chrissie looked up. "Me?" She could hardly get the words out.

"Let's hear how well you play."

Mr. Bird was next to her now, staring down at her.

"I can't—"

"You can laugh enough," he said. "Let's hear . . ."

Chrissie put the fife up to her lips.

Her mouth was dry.

She could hardly get her breath.

She curled her fingers around the fife.

She blew into it.

Not a sound.

She tried again.

A small, squeaky sound came out.

"Out," said Mr. Bird.

Chrissie looked at the gym doors.

They looked far away.

She right-flanked across the room, swinging her arms.

She'd never let Mr. Bird know she cared.

♪ CHAPTER 7 ♪

Chrissie rushed down the street. Her fife was under one arm. Thankly was under the other.

She had captured him halfway down the block . . . just turning into Mrs. Niebling's path.

He was scratching at her arm as hard as he could.

Any minute, she'd have to let him go.

She climbed her front steps. She didn't stop to sniff at the wreath.

She pushed the door open.

Thankly jumped out of her arms. He streaked up the stairs.

Chrissie could hear her mother moving around in the kitchen.

She didn't want to see her mother though.

What would she say?

Her father was taking the day off to see her and Teresa at the Sunrise Mall.

Her mother was going to skip one of her classes at the college.

She started up the stairs.

What would the professor think when he heard . . .

"Is that you, Chrissie?" her mother called. She came down the hall, a spoon in her hand. A little dab of cookie batter was smeared on her mouth.

She smiled at Chrissie. "The perfect person to help me with my cookies."

"I don't—" Chrissie began.

"I'm making thumbprints," she said. "And your thumbs are the perfect size."

Chrissie dropped her jacket on the stairs. She followed her mother into the kitchen.

On the table was a tray. It was filled with dabs of cookie dough.

Chrissie stood there pressing her thumb into the centers.

Her mother dipped a bit of jelly into each. "Isn't it great you're home to do this," her mother said. "Cookie baking is the best part of Christmas."

Chrissie nodded a little.

"Whoops," said her mother. "Something's wrong. I thought you'd say the best part was the present part."

Chrissie didn't answer. She thought about Willie. Better to give than receive.

If she said one word, she knew she'd cry. What had the professor said? *Nothing like "Jingle Bells" on the fife.*

Too late now.

She'd never learn it.

She'd never have to.

She'd never march.

Never . . .

The front door burst open.

Teresa was home from practice.

She came into the kitchen.

"Cookies," she said slowly. "Nice. Chrissie's thumb is the perfect size."

Her mother looked at Teresa and then at Chrissie. "Just what I said."

"Listen—" Teresa began.

"I think I'd better do my homework," said Chrissie. She started out of the kitchen.

Her mother reached out. "Tell me—"

Chrissie raced up the stairs.

Behind her she could hear Teresa talking.

She went into her bedroom and closed the door.

For a minute she looked out the window.

It was almost dark outside.

She could see Mrs. Aiello's Christmas lights blinking.

She slid down on the floor.

The edge of Thankly's tail was sticking out from under the spread.

She reached under her bed for him . . . and pulled back.

He had almost taken a chunk out of her finger.

She looked underneath. Thankly's eyes were big and green and angry.

"Too bad for you, Thankly." She leaned her head back against the spread.

A moment later Joseph opened the door. He was carrying a paper bag.

"Spring Flowers." He opened the bag.

It was the huge moose bottle.

Chrissie didn't say anything.

She could see he was waiting though.

"Alysia will love it," she said.

Joseph smiled. "I was going to quit as soon as I bought this. But guess what?"

"What?"

"I'm going to stay some more. I'll buy the same thing for Mom."

"You're good, Joseph. Really good."

Chrissie closed her eyes. If only Mr. Bird were like Joseph. And Mrs. Niebling.

She looked out the window. She could see a reflection of the blinking lights. Red, then blue, then green. Red again . . .

If only she were like Joseph.

"Mom said I could come up to see how you were doing," he said.

"Don't say anything."

He raised his hands up. "Not me. I'm not talking. I'm just sitting here."

Chrissie had to smile. At the same time, she could feel tears in her eyes.

Joseph cleared his throat. "Teresa told me you were laughing at Mr. Bird. You and Willie."

Chrissie watched as one of Thankly's paws came out from under the spread.

Thankly was hunting her.

Any minute he'd attack.

"Willie was making parrot noises," she said. "I couldn't stop laughing . . ."

She touched the top of Thankly's paw gently.

"I'm out of the band," she said.

"Willie too?"

Chrissie shook her head. "Willie is good. Willie is great at the drums. I can't even play two notes without squeaking."

"You didn't try hard enough," Joseph said.

"I did so." Chrissie swallowed. She couldn't get the professor out of her mind. He'd be so disappointed.

"Poor Professor Thum-de-dum," Chrissie said. "He won't even be at the mall to-morrow night."

"Learn it now," Joseph said.

"Too late."

"Learn it anyway. Learn it for the professor," he said.

"He loves 'Jingle Bells' on the fife." Chrissie stopped. "But I . . ."

"In football," Joseph said, "you do the same thing over and over. And then when you think you'll never know it—"

"I'm no good at—" Chrissie began.

"—you stop thinking about it. It happens, and you feel as if you always knew it."

"Maybe," Chrissie said.

Joseph stood up. "It's supper time."

Chrissie nodded. "I'm coming."

She waited until Joseph went downstairs.

Then she looked around. She didn't even know where she had put the fife.

♪ CHAPTER 8 ♩

It was Saturday morning.

No one else was home.

Her father and mother were Christmas shopping.

Joseph had a game.

Teresa was out buying hair ribbons before playing at the mall this afternoon.

Chrissie wondered where Thankly was.

He must be in the house. She had seen him somewhere.

She looked down at her hands.

There were little round circles of red on her fingers.

That was from practicing.

She had started after supper last night.

She had played "Jingle Bells" a hundred times. A thousand.

Teresa was having a fit, screaming that she had to study . . . yelling she couldn't stand it anymore . . . that it was too late.

And in the beginning, that's what "Jingle Bells" sounded like when Chrissie played: too-late-now, too-late-now.

Then, by bedtime, the sound changed to not-so-bad, not-so-bad.

She tried it again right now.

Her lips were sore.

But the sound had changed again.

It wasn't squeaky anymore.

It sounded like bells.

She could picture a sleigh, and the snow,

and even though she wasn't in the band, even though she wouldn't get to wear the wide blue ribbon and play this afternoon . . . she was beginning to love the sound of the fife.

She went to her closet.

She shrugged on her jacket.

She grabbed her fife and went down-stairs.

She'd have to do this fast . . . before she didn't have any courage left.

Her hands were damp from thinking about what she was going to do.

She made herself think about the pro-fessor though.

She had to do it.

She passed the living room.

Thankly was stretched out under the couch.

He opened one eye as she came down the stairs.

"I'll be right back," she said.

She opened the front door.

Before she could close it again, there was a flash of gray.

Thankly was out the door.

"Good grief, Thankly," she yelled. "Get back in here."

Tail up, Thankly streaked away.

At least he wasn't going toward Mrs. Niebling's.

She should go after him.

It would take her hours though.

Thankly would be over fences, under bushes, in tight little corners.

No, she was going straight to the professor's house.

"Stay away from Mrs. Niebling," she shouted after him. Then she hurried down the street.

The professor had a neat house, with little stones up along the front path.

The professor's wife let her in, smiling.

Their Christmas tree was neat too. In among the lights were bells. They hung on red ribbons.

"Reindeer bells." The professor's wife reached out to shake a branch.

Chrissie wondered what to say.

How could she tell the professor's wife she had come to play the fife?

She didn't have to say anything though.

"Come into the living room," the professor's wife said.

The professor was sitting on the couch.

He looked almost the same. His gray hair and mustache were flying all over the place.

He was wearing a bathrobe. It was a gray one that almost matched his hair.

He smiled. "Here's our best little marcher," he said.

She saw he was talking to someone else.

She turned. In a corner chair, dressed in orange and green, was Mr. Bird.

He looked surprised to see her . . . as surprised as she was.

The professor's wife was smiling. "I'll bring a snack," she said.

"She likes to feed people," the professor said.

Chrissie tried to hide the fife behind her back. She had to get out of there.

"I'm sorry you can't come tonight," she said. She edged her way back to the door.

The professor looked sad. "I know."

She bumped into the Christmas tree.

The professor put his hand out. "Did you come to play for me?"

She shook her head. "No, I just—"

"Would you bring my fife?" the professor called to his wife.

He smiled at Chrissie. "This is the nicest Christmas present I could have."

♪ CHAPTER 9 ♪

Chrissie raced back toward her house.

The professor was right. There was nothing like "Jingle Bells" on the fife.

Willie and Michelle were right too. You had to listen for the sound.

Joseph was right. She was glad she had played for the professor.

She smiled thinking of Willie . . . better to give than receive.

It was almost like that.

" 'Oh, what fun it is to ride . . .' " she sang. She twirled around the telephone pole. She felt wonderful.

She and the professor had played "Jingle Bells" about nineteen times.

"Wonderful," the professor said each time. "Let's do it again."

He said it even when she made mistakes.

And she had made a couple.

Maybe he hadn't even noticed.

Somewhere in the middle, Mr. Bird had waved and left.

Afterward, they had cookies and juice, and the professor had told her how hard it was for him to learn "Silent Night."

"It was 'Squeaky Night,' " he said, "for a long time."

"Look at him," the professor's wife had said when Chrissie was leaving. "He's almost better. You've made him better."

"Have a good time at the mall," the professor called after her.

Chrissie turned the corner. She started down the next street.

She had meant to tell him about the band. She couldn't though.

Mr. Bird would tell him.

She didn't want to think about that.

She passed Mrs. Niebling's house and looked around.

Thankly wasn't there.

She could see Mrs. Niebling in her living room, though.

She stood there for a moment.

Then she knew what she was going to do.

She raced home.

Thankly was waiting at the door.

He slipped in ahead of her.

Chrissie was inside just for a minute.

Then she was out again, heading back to Mrs. Niebling's house.

Willie was running up the street, two blocks away. He waved and yelled something.

She didn't stop though.

She rang Mrs. Niebling's bell.

Mrs. Niebling opened the door just a crack. "Come in," she said. "Hurry. I don't want all the cold air in here."

Chrissie went inside.

The Christmas tree sparkled with lights that looked like candles, and old silvery ornaments.

Chrissie held out her own ornament, the lady with the flowers. "I brought you this," she said.

Mrs. Niebling didn't say anything for a moment. Then she took the ornament. She hung it carefully on a high branch.

When she turned back, Chrissie could see tears in her pale blue eyes.

"I'm sorry about Thankly," Chrissie said.

"I thought of something. I could get him a bell. Hang it around his neck."

Mrs. Niebling stood there, nodding a little.

Chrissie tried to think of something else to say. "Like reindeers . . ." she began.

Just then the doorbell rang.

It was a long ring.

Someone was holding his finger over the bell.

It had to be Willie.

Mrs. Niebling went to the door. "Don't let the cold air in," she said in her cranky voice.

"I need Chrissie," he said. "Right away please. It's important."

Chrissie said good-bye to Mrs. Niebling. Then she hurried outside.

"Hurry," he yelled. "You're back in the band. I saw Mr. Bird."

Chrissie came down the steps.

"He said to tell you he didn't want to say anything in front of the professor."

Chrissie felt a lump in her throat.

She stood there for another minute.

"I have to change, and comb my hair, and . . ." she began.

She waved at Mrs. Niebling. Mrs. Niebling was smiling at her.

Then she turned toward Willie.

"Let's get going," she said. "We don't have all day."